GOOD NIGHT, GORILLA

Peggy Rathmann

SCHOLASTIC INC.
New York   Toronto   London   Auckland   Sydney

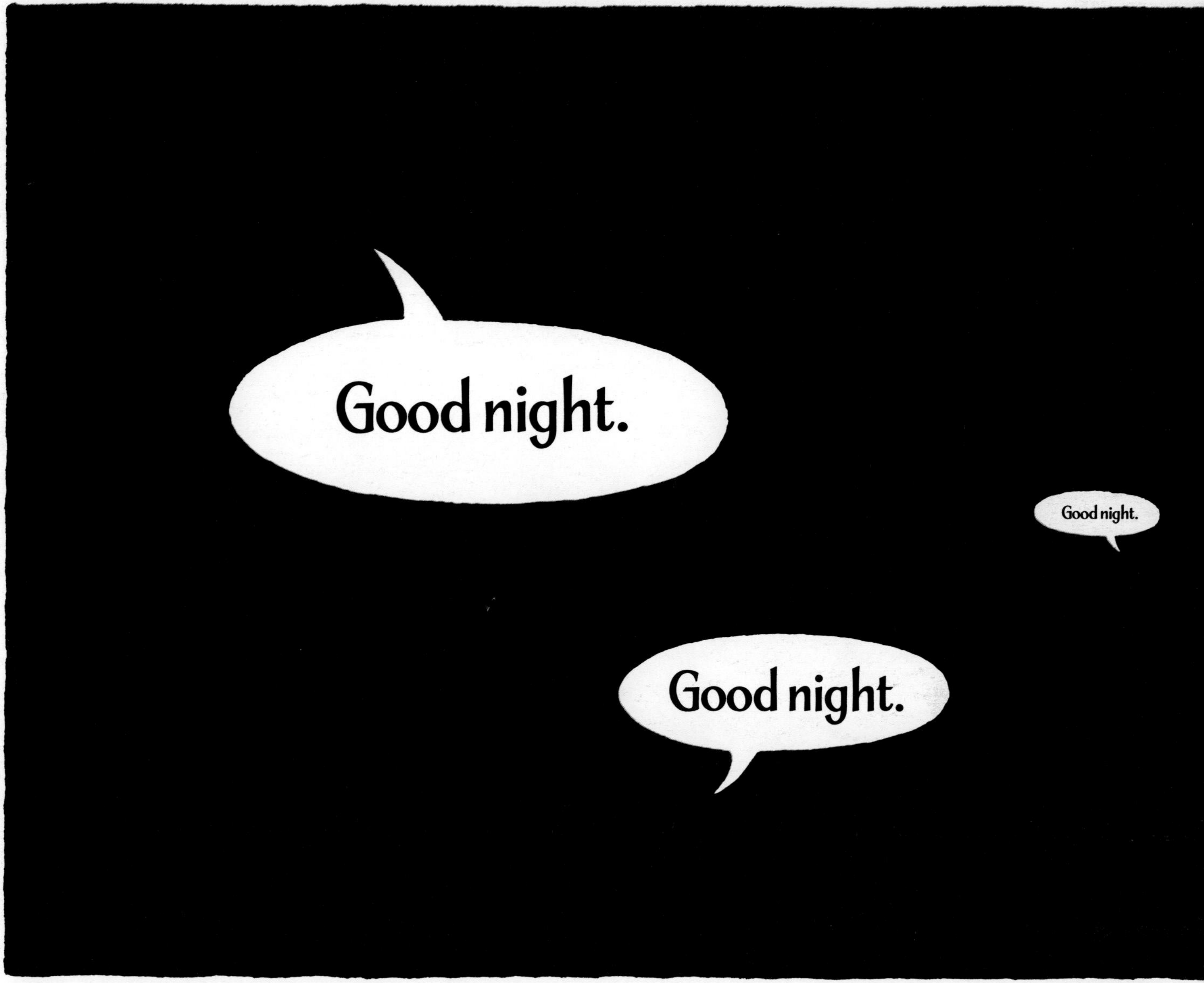
Good night.
Good night.
Good night.

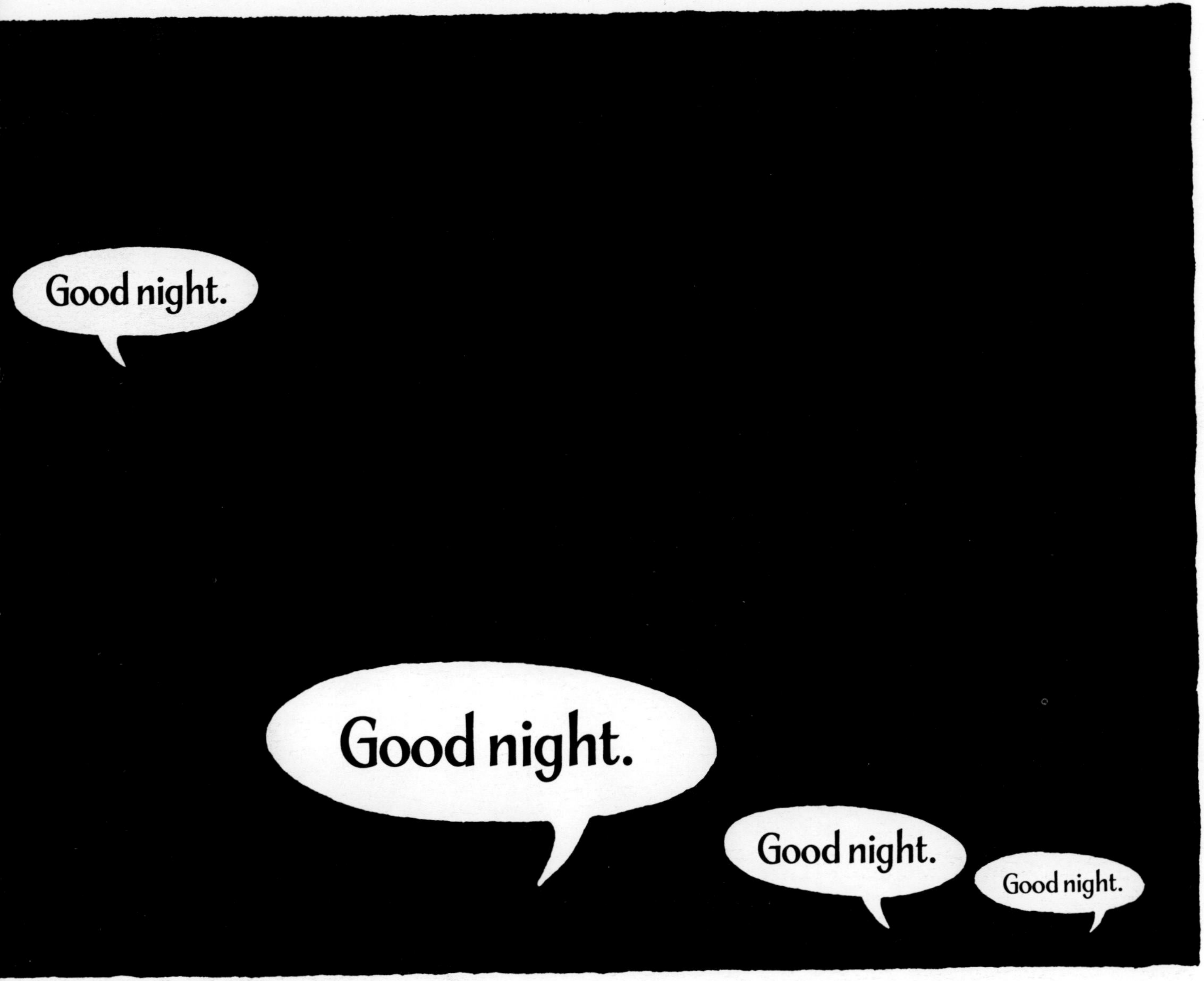
Good night.
Good night.
Good night.
Good night.

**For Mr. and Mrs. Joseph McQuaid,
and all their little gorillas**

ISBN 0-545-09619-7

Text and illustrations copyright © 1994 by Peggy Rathmann.
All rights reserved. Published by Scholastic Inc.,
555 Broadway, New York, NY 10012,
by arrangement with G. P. Putnam's Sons,
a division of The Putnam & Grosset Group.

10 9 8 7 6 5 4 3 2 1   08 09 10 11 12 13/0

Printed in the U.S.A.   23

First Scholastic printing, September 1995

Lettering by David Gatti